touch

touch

by Adania Shibli
translated from the Arabic by Paula Haydar

clockroot books

First published in the United States in 2010 by

Clockroot Books
An imprint of Interlink Publishing Group, Inc.
46 Crosby Street
Northampton, Massachusetts 01060
www.clockrootbooks.com
www.interlinkbooks.com

Library of Congress Cataloging-in-Publication Data
Shibli, 'Adaniyah.
[Masaas. English]
Touch / by Adania Shibli ; translated from the Arabic by Paula Haydar.
—— 1st American ed.
    p. cm.
ISBN 978-1-56656-807-4 (pbk.)
I. Haydar, Paula, 1965- II. Title.
PJ7962.H425M5713 2010
892.7'37——dc22

                        2009048867

The quotation from the Quran (ya sin 37) on page 13 is from the Arberry translation.

Cover painting © Elena Ray
Book design by Juliana Spear

Printed and bound in the United States of America

contents

colors

1

The big brown water tank stood on four legs, appearing from a distance to be an ant standing perfectly still.

Once it had been another color, which lasted until a tiny spot of rust came, and grew and grew until it took over the whole tank and turned it brown.

Behind one of the legs of the tank stood a little girl. The brown covering her, though, was not caused by that spot of rust, but by the tailor who, making a dress for the mother, did not use up all of the heavy, brown wool laced every so often with golden thread. A small piece had been left that was just enough to make a small dress.

The little girl's eyes were fixed on the leg in front of her. Rust was dangling from it in tiny squares and pieces, making it look rough. She stretched out her hand and pressed it on the leg. She heard a delicate sound as the pieces of cold rust broke off. She let go of the leg, and some of the rust splinters fell to the ground, while others stuck to her hand.

The splinters on her hand were still cold, so she carried them out from the shade of the tank to warm them up a little. Out of the shade, there appeared, in addition to the little brown splinters of rust, little dots all over her hand, sparkling.

Gold.

In the sun, the brown and gold dots made a delicate, transparent glove that matched the small dress.

The other hand did not hold anything. It stayed firmly closed, just as it was. She opened it, and it was wet with sweat. When she put it in the sun, it too sparkled with dots and threads of gold. She rubbed her hand onto one of the tank legs again to add a little more brown and sparkle to it, but instead of gold the roughness of the rust stuck to her hand; a roughness similar to the roughness of her woolen dress.

The little girl stood behind the water tank on her way to have a pee. Silence enveloped everything. She would not hold her dress up to pee, because one hand had the glove and the other was rough and hurting. So the urine began its double-streamed path down her legs on its own. She stood there in the sun, playing with the brown and the gold on her dress and hand while the pee on her legs dried.

A little girl gets her hand dirty and then pees on her leg.

2

The little girl sat on top of the bales of hay stacked in the back of the pickup. Inside, the father was driving up the mountain.

From the peak of the mountain a rainbow emerged, stretching across the sky all the way to the plains, and disappearing.

Sometimes colors disappeared from nature, and all that remained was green on the mountain, yellow on the hay, and blue on the sky in summer. Before the end of the spring, the green and red crayons got used up because there were so many anemones, yet it seemed the pink crayon would last through many winters.

When they reached the peak of the mountain, its point was gone. The peak was as flat as all the other fields and on it stood a lone building. The father got out of the car and quickly disappeared between the statues and the trees behind the fence of the building.

The girl stayed out sitting on the hay, waiting for him.

The longest-lasting crayon would be the purple one. Only one violet would appear then disappear, and there was one rainbow, which would also disappear.

Now that the peak was no longer a point, the girl went searching for the place from which the rainbow had chosen to emerge.

So many colors were everywhere and on the windows of the building. From a distance, the little squares of color on one of the windows formed the shape of a man on a horse slaying a dragon, and closer up a picture of a wolf hanging on the wall, and beneath it the father was sitting next to a woman.

The girl walked off toward the trees, continuing her search for the traces of the rainbow. Beneath the trees nothing but wispy, dry leaves gathered. Their crunching underfoot was the only sound on top of the mountain, until a breeze came, shuddering other leaves and bringing the sun closer to the end of the sky.

Around, all the trees and the paths looked alike, so the little girl followed the path of the sun's movement, chasing after it so that it would not get dark and all the colors disappear. Then she started to run, faster and faster until she reached the edge of the mountain.

And there, from the edge of the mountain, the sky stretched out to the distant fields, while the sun was about to disappear, dragging behind it a long ray of purple, the last color of the day.

A rainbow appears, then when it starts to disappear the girl runs to see it from a good spot. The father shows up, which I think is referring to her dad.

3

Everyone managed to find black outfits to wear, except the little girl. The search for a black outfit for her, followed by an attempt to improvise one, nearly made the family forget their grief, so it was decided that this task should be left to her.

The closet door was always half open, because no one fixed it or showed any interest in fixing it.

The girl removed all the clothes from the closet and placed them in the small space between the closet on one side and the beds on the other. The pile of clothes remained multicolored, despite what the constantly angry art teacher said, that all colors mixed together would make white.

A pair of dark blue velvet pants and a wool sweater that had in addition to the dark blue other little colors won the almost-black outfit contest. After she put them on, she found a hole in the pants near the left knee.

On the way to the mosque, she bought a bottle of cola with a red ribbon on it. The liquid inside it was black, or closer to black than to any other color around her. She continued on her way, holding the bottle in her right hand and hiding the hole in her pants with her left.

She was the last to arrive at the square of the mosque. When she got there, she found that the mother had fainted and had been taken to an ambulance parked out back, so she headed in that direction.

The back door of the ambulance was open, but she could not get to it, because a huge crowd of women in black created an immense wall between her and the door. She could not even get a glimpse of the mother's shoes. As the crowd of women in black got bigger and bigger, she, in her dark blue clothes, got pushed further and further back, unable to resist. Her right hand was holding the bottle and her left was covering the hole. She could not remove her hand, or everyone would see the hole.

The pushing became harder and harsher, and each time it would force her hand away from the hole, so she would press on it harder and harder, using all her strength, including that in her right hand. That hand now had weakened its hold on the bottle, and a little black liquid leaked out with each step she was pushed backward.

At the end of the square, the wall of the mosque rose behind the girl, keeping her from getting pushed back any further. She stood there looking toward the ambulance, which had no white left, after the black drape of women wrapped it. But above, on top of the ambulance, the red light kept spinning inside itself, not veiled by anything, switching regularly from dark red to light red. She waited for its regular return to dark red, so that it would look like the red label on the empty bottle in her hand.

The girl puts on dark clothes and walks toward a mosque. The mother faints.

4

When something shiny appeared in the distance, it was the neighbor's eyes. In the fields, his eyes were green.

The little girl lay down on the green grass and the neighbor got closer until he was on top of her. From behind, the blue sky enveloped him, and his eyes enveloped their own blueness.

He got so close that his features blurred, but their noses kept them from getting any closer. The two bodies were tangled together as one.

The neighbor was lying on the hard soil. In winter, the hard soil was muddy and flowed under their bodies. His eyes were brown.

He put his hand on her neck while her hand was on the soil, then she lifted it to his eyes. His hand moved along her neck while hers went back and forth over his eyes. His fingers pressed hard on her neck and her fingers pressed hard on his eyes, and she hurt him. He moved away, not wanting to play *evol* with her anymore.

They went back home together, and behind them the gray dust rose up covering all the plants, but his eyes did not turn gray; they were shining again.

The little girl went up a side path that took her farther and farther from the neighbor until he disappeared.

As she walked, something shiny again appeared in the distance beneath a dusty tree and she approached it.

In the shade, a snake lay in the gray dust, which enveloped it from all sides, yet it was still shining.

8

A guy was grabbing a girl by the neck before they were playing a game.

5

The mother rolled the sleeves of her dress up to her elbows, and the gold bracelets appeared. The little girl undressed and sat on the bathroom floor, hugging herself tightly and watching the cold bracelets.

Three times for the hair. Three times for the body.

The mother used to bathe her, until the dream came. The mother was lying in the neighbors' courtyard on her right side with her dress lifted all the way to the top of her white legs. The old neighbor stood at her feet, and his wife behind him. In his hand he had a knife he used to stab the mother's left leg all over, but there was no blood; the places he stabbed her simply turned blue. The mother laughed and the neighbor laughed and his wife, too, while the mother's leg was covered with blue spots and lines.

The girl no longer ran before the mother to the bathroom, nor did she bathe anymore, until the eighth sister came and led her.

The mother put the pot of water down and went out, leaving the two of them alone together.

They got undressed and approached the pot of hot water. The eighth sister picked up the plastic cup, filled it with water from the pot, and poured the water over her hair. Then she filled it again and poured the water over her body. She refilled the cup once more, and held it with one hand while the other gripped the bar of soap and lathered her hair. Now and then she poured water from the cup over her head onto her hair and the white suds would disappear, but not

The girl has a nightmare about her mother.

9

completely. Some would stay and others would roll down her back and if they did not disappear they would continue on their path, along the water, down the bathroom floor, advancing from one tile to another, sometimes easily and sometimes with difficulty, depending on how the eighth sister poured the water. In the meantime, the cup stayed in her right hand. Originally the cup had been blue, but it had started to turn white from the scratches it got falling on the floor, and now it was even whiter because of the soap foam stuck to it.

The spots of cold reached every part of the little girl's body, while she waited her turn to hold the cup. She reached to take it from the eighth sister's hand, but the sister moved it away from her. The little girl then lunged at it, but instead of grabbing the cup, she bumped into the pot and tipped it over, spilling all the hot water. The eighth sister pushed her down into the water mixed with soap and dirt and cold.

They battled in silence.

The little girl bathed with cold water from the faucet. Once for the hair, once for the body, no soap either time. The pain of the cold water eased the pain of the blows.

The next day, all the places she'd been hit turned into blue spots and lines on her arms and chest and lots on her legs.

Little girl gets in a fight with eighth sister

6

The peeling of the house paint was at its peak, yet no one noticed, having gotten used to the gradual transformation of the colors. Looking at the veranda from the front door, it was clear that the paint on its walls was peeling, while the scenery it overlooked was not.

The peeling paint looked like a burned hand, swollen and inflamed. The little girl moved closer to one of the veranda posts and scraped her fingernails against the most swollen part. A little piece of paint got lodged under her fingernail, but the expression on her face and her closed eyes were caused by the sun that struck her when she looked up to remove the piece of paint. And she forgot about that piece of paint when through her lids she saw the color orange covering everything. When she opened her eyes, everything became as it had been, so she quickly closed them and again the world turned orange.

The sun was very close, and the girl felt its heat touch her head, then her body. She turned around toward the door. The mother was next to it, standing at the washing machine. On hot days, the mother gathered all the dirty laundry, creating multicolored piles around her. The girl shut her eyes again in order to see nothing but orange all over the world, but the washing machine started, repeating its monotonous tune. Its sound had taken over now. She left the veranda and hid inside the father's car.

When she shut her eyes inside the car, the orange did not return.

More than half the day passed, and the shadows grew longer again and the washing almost dried as the little girl went on watching the empty courtyard in the little rearview mirror that hung in the middle of the car, shutting her eyes from time to time, hoping the orange would return.

In the midst of that hot silence, a car appeared in the mirror. It turned around in the courtyard and then parked in the shade.

The doors were opened and shut behind four people. The youngest among them was wearing an orange shirt.

The girl kept closing her eyes and seeing orange

7

The departure of the sun allowed the darkness to stretch its black over everything the girl looked at.

Black swallowed all the colors. She lit the lantern in the room, and the white paint jumped into it while the blackness stood on the windowsill, carelessly filling in the spaces between the window's bars.

"And a sign for them is the night; we strip it of the day and lo, they are in darkness."

She put the little Quran, with its fine pages like candy wrappers, under her mattress and turned off the light. And lo, they are in darkness.

Before the sun was created, black alone filled the universe. Black was there before creation. Before she was born. And after she would die, blackness would return to its place, her empty place.

So God was behind the darkness, unfolding it and folding it again whichever way He willed.

She talks about darkness

8

When she opened the window in the dark room, the girl discovered that it was still daylight, and everything within the window frame appeared pale, as if the colors were in a coma. She moved her eyes away from the window and went for a walk.

She walked with her head down, her eyes gazing at the uniformity of color in the various streets. Except for a colored piece of garbage here and there, the street was a world painted in black and white. Here was a slightly darker black spot from either oil or urine, surrounded by other much smaller spots. There was a white piece of gum that had been run over by cars and people's feet until it turned gray. And between here and there were bits of glass that were scattered following an accident that had begun with two parallel pitch-black lines made by brakes trying to stop the tires from rolling, but failing. The girl looked behind to see if she had left any traces herself.

The street stretched on all the way to a certain spot, most of which was covered with white petals.

The girl raised her head and saw a tall almond tree planted behind a high wall. Over time its branches had crept over the wall and spread over the street. The branches were covered by white flowers with sky blue filling the spaces between them.

The borders of her wedding dress blended into the wall behind her, but now, against the black of the street and the blue of the sky, the white could be seen.

silence

I

Noise

Waves of sound moved toward the little girl, each trying to be the first to reach her ears and fall on them like a hammer pounding, and her ears opened wide to welcome them. After her brother's scream, she heard the fly, and after it flew away, she heard the hum of the electric meter.

In the entire world there was not a single moment of silence.

The sounds that stormed her ears would not come out. They piled on top of each other. She poked her finger into her ear to try to pick them out, but failed. She tried sitting behind others, so their ears would pick up the coming sounds instead of hers, to prevent the sounds from piling up there, but the sounds wanted all the ears.

The heat was intense, and as on every hot day, the washing machine stubbornly repeated its monotonous sound, with the mother beside it. The girl searched for some silence to find comfort in, but before she could the pain found its way to her ears. She blocked them, but then she heard the sound of blocking them, which was like the sound of the sea, so it only worsened the pain that had turned into illness.

Then she collapsed.

After a while, after her body turned into flames, the sounds stopped coming, even the sound of the mother drawing cold water and pouring it over her burning body. The movement of the mother's lips equaled the stillness of the father's lips as the three of them traveled together.

When they got to a white room, the father moved the girl from his arms to the high bed. The doctor lifted her dress, so she pushed his hand back as hard as she could muster in her weakness. He took a little light and looked inside her ears, to see the sounds that went in but did not come out. Her lips trembled.

The doctor said, without her able to hear him, she was suffering from a severe infection in the ears; they had brought her there just in time. She could have lost her hearing for good, if they had come any later. This kind of illness would come back her whole life, he said, because they had come a little bit late. This is what the mother tells her every time this illness recurs.

Could've lost hearing for good

On the way back, the mother moved her mouth angrily without stopping, while the father gripped the steering wheel without moving it or his lips much. Silence hung on the stillness of the father's lips, and on the silence hung the little girl's eyes.

2

Lonliness

The sharp whistling sound that overtook the little girl's ears signaled the collapse and the collapse signaled the filling up of her ears with sounds. When she got up, her body was a dry leaf withered in the heat.

The girl lay on her bed inside the silence, and the mother beside her every once in a while put oily drops in her ears. After several days the mother took her to the doctor, who sent them to the nurse. The nurse wrapped a plastic apron around the girl, attaching a cold metal saucer to her neck below her ears. Then he pushed the biggest syringe in the world into her ear and water began to flow in torrents in and out and onto the metal saucer resting on her shoulder. After that, the paradise of silence disappeared and the world of sounds returned.

At home the noise was constant, never stopping except during the mother's prayer, or in front of the locked door to the bedroom of the mother and the father. Even the television set participated in the family's humility, but prayer was short and soon the door would be reopened. There was no escape except to escape from all the possibilities of noise and illness, and to search for silence.

The girl stopped sharing meals with her siblings, as these meals involved more screaming than food. She started eating alone, then sleeping alone in the living room, because the screaming followed the sisters into the bedroom. Later, her father built a wall between her bed and the guests, since the guests had even louder voices than her siblings.

But the sounds still crept in to her room through the hole in the door, and the space between the bottom of the door and the floor, and between the top of the door and the doorframe, and from everywhere.

During the day she wandered far into the fields, and in the evening she sat in the father's car until everyone fell asleep. Then she would come inside, put the car keys on top of the fireplace, and go into her bedroom until the next sound came and pushed her out of the house.

Loneliness always saved a place for the little girl inside the silence.

3
E V o L

The father sat cross-legged on the multicolored rug with all the stripes, his long legs reaching more than halfway around the circular tray, while the little girl's legs barely enclosed the rest of it. The sound of cucumbers crunching in her father's mouth stretched over the tray between them.

Then they headed to the car.

The car transported them to wherever, engulfing them in its silence and isolation as changing images flashed across its windows. The car's silence extended all the way to the end of the road and into their courtyard.

The courtyard remained quiet until it began to fill up on the right-hand side with the sisters coming to play or to fight, either way accompanied by noise, so the little girl had to withdraw into the car and watch them in the rearview mirror. Their voices penetrated the glass from the distance, like whispers.

In the corner of the little mirror, the seventh sister stood near two stones, a small stick balanced between them. She was holding a big stick, which she brought toward the little stick. She looked up, then at the stick, then up, then at the stick, then up, and she swung at the little stick with the big stick. Up the little stick flew, across the mirror, passing beyond it, then disappearing, as did her sisters after it.

They went on like that, appearing and disappearing after the little stick, until the rain came and sent them into the house.

The first drops of rain fell loud on the roof of the car. Yet the heavier the rain became, the softer its sound became, like whispers. From inside the car, the wetness and sounds seemed far away, whereas at school, when it rained outside, the noise stayed inside the classroom. The only silence came after a soft knock on the door, behind which the neighbor appeared carrying her coat.

The children at school all said the neighbor was in love with her.

The rain stopped. She opened the car door and shut her eyes against the cold, burning wind. She walked across the courtyard, then through the mud, until she reached the tree behind the neighbor's house and waited there for him to come outside.

They walked together through the mud, then across the courtyard, to the car. After they locked the car door behind them, it started to rain again, and they started playing in silence.

A hand reached for the other's body as quickly as the seventh sister's hand swung at the little stick. She put her hand on his. She put her hand on his face. He put his hand on her leg. She put her hand on his hair. He put his hand on her back. She put her hands inside his shirt above his chest. Her hand heard the noise of his heart, which again disappeared when she moved her hand away.

They played and played until the end of the rain. The little girl never put her hand back on the neighbor's heart again, so that silence could keep their game of *evol* a secret.

4 The dead Brother

The little girl stood on the edge of the veranda, hugging the paint-chipped post beside her, her hair covered with the mother's headscarf, and her eyes glued to the distant street where the sounds seemed to have disappeared.

After seventeen cars passed, the brother would come. One, two, three, four, five, six, seven, eight, nine, ten, eleven, twelve, thirteen, she was not sure if the brother would come, fourteen, fifteen, if only he would come, sixteen, maybe he would not, seventeen. The blare of an ambulance siren pierced the scarf over her ears.

The whistle of the siren in her ears was as soft as the first ripples of a wave. The closer it got to shore, the rougher and louder it became, as did the roar of the women.

The ambulance arrived in the courtyard.

She pressed her face against the post, despite the roughness of its peeling paint, her eyes still glued to the rear door of the ambulance, which was going to open and the brother was going to jump out and fly to the veranda so he could rip the scarf off her ears and scream as loud as he could into them and then she would die.

The door opened, but the brother did not jump out. Instead, he was carried out and rushed into the house.

A short while, then she snuck in there.

The mother was sitting on the multicolored rug with all the stripes, her legs encircling the brother's motionless head. The rest of his body was covered in an ironed white sheet with pale brown squares. Silence engulfed him. Not a single sound from him anymore.

The little girl listened very closely to the dead brother, but silence was all there was of him, forever.

5

Imperfect memory [handwritten]

The mother opened the closet, which hid two small drawers. The top drawer was the father's, and was full of socks; the second drawer was the mother's, and was not full.

The little girl did not go near the big closet. Instead she remained in the father's bed, watching from far off what was happening. But the mother's black outfits made it impossible for her to see anything. All that reached her were the sounds of the hand searching inside the second drawer and the jingle of the gold bracelets on the wrist.

When the mother finally turned around, there was a small picture between her fingers.

A few days later, the brother's small picture was transformed into a big one that was hung on the wall above the television set, in defiance of death.

The bedroom door was open and rectangular, so the little girl was able to watch television from her bed until the last moment of wakefulness.

If the television was on, she did not take her eyes off it. But when death came, the picture left the television and instead, the brother's picture settled in above it.

For some time now, her eyes had been staring at the still picture, in which they saw and would continue to see forever her brother's crooked necktie, because he hadn't taken more time, not much, to fix it.

If only the left side of the tie were lowered just a little. She shut her eyes to hurry herself to sleep, then opened them again.

The bedroom door was rectangular and straight. In the center was the television, and above the television was the picture with the chaos of the crooked necktie.

She tilted her head, and the entire rectangle of the door tilted too, but the necktie was still crooked. If only the television were on, its moving pictures might prevail over her brother's still one.

She slid to the edge of the bed so that her head hung off and she could tilt it more and straighten the necktie, but the rectangle tilted more, and the tie still did not straighten.

She slid her whole body halfway off the bed so she could tilt as much as she wanted. She put one hand firmly on the floor to support her body in its new position. Now she saw that things were not just tilted, but about to collapse. The television wanted to fall off the table, the table wanted to come into her room, the rectangle of the door was about to fall and take the picture with it, shattering the glass, and the shards were going to scatter everywhere on the floor, reaching her hand, and the glass between her fingers was going to be cold and hurt and bleed. She lifted her hand up off the floor and quickly her body fell off the bed.

A weak sound emerged, carrying the tidings of weeping across the silence of the house. A black shadow jumped into the rectangle in front of her, hiding the television and the picture.

The sixth sister lifted the girl back onto the bed and walked over to the television set. She turned it on, turning the sound all the way down, so as not to wake the family with such disrespect for the dead brother.

The little girl remained in her bed, and watched through the rectangle of the doorway the changing pictures on the television. Every once in a while she looked over at the sixth sister, who had sat down with her, sharing the silence.

6
Colors and Silence

A car drove around in the courtyard of the house searching for some shade.

The first foot appeared and landed on the dirt, then the second foot, until there were eight.

The four were still wandering around silently in the courtyard, waiting for the family to notice them, not noticing the little girl sitting in her deepest silence inside the father's car. She saw them in the mirror and then went outside to them. When she crossed in front of them, silence persisted.

She went behind the door of the house; then there appeared from behind it the mother and the fourth and the fifth sisters, and the girl hardly visible behind, to greet the four housepainters. After that the housepainters came every morning.

Love occurred in secret, but it became apparent when the oldest son listened more intently than the others to the fourth sister as she explained about the colors and which should go where in the rooms. Her voice, as cool as morning mist, entered only his ears.

The morning disappeared and so did the fourth sister, until noon, when the fifth sister brought lunch on the piled-up tray, walking as if everything under her feet were smooth and straight. The mother filled the bowls to just below the top of the faces of the prince and princess that were painted inside the rim of the bowl. And even though the way was long and tricky, the food, even the soup, never rose above the two faces of the prince and princess.

The middle son met the fifth sister halfway, where no one else was, with only the steam of the food separating the two faces.

The fifth sister held the tray in her hands at two points, and he came nearer and shared them with her. The paint was always dry on his hands, so it did not leave any traces on her hands when they made the exchange, careful not to let anything spill out of the bowls. Each hand rested upon the other until they slowly separated, moving in opposite directions, love growing stronger.

The girl did not carry the big food tray or the little coffee tray, but still she waited every day for love to happen with the youngest son, moving her waiting from the house to the father's car, which was parked beside *his* father's car. Yet it did not come.

On one of the painting nights, she waited for morning to arrive so she could ask the painters to paint the rooms orange like his shirt, but they painted everything white.

The tray was clean and the tea was neatly in the little cups. The girl carried them with caution that turned into slowness in hope of turning into love. She got halfway there, but the young painter was not there to meet her. Her hands shook with fatigue. The rest of the way was full of colors spilling in all directions, and she tried not to step on them. And the way became longer as she walked along the streams of paint and the paint buckets and the brushes. The closer she got to the painters, the more her hands shook. At the point of meeting, there was not any tea left in the cups.

The little girl walked outside the house and started whistling, trying to force the sound into her ears so she would get sick and die far away from all eyes and all ears.

The whistling ate up her breath, so she stopped to fill up with air, which had the taste of paint. During the time it took her to inhale, another whistle suddenly entered. She looked around to find where it was coming from and did not see a mouth anywhere. But it was coming from the rooms that were being painted. The two went on whistling, day after day, until the last day of painting.

Then silence returned, putting an end to love.

7

a Silent prayer

The young girl dreamed that her body was floating up to the sky while she remained below, looking at the road, which started with a demolished building transforming into a withered grapevine. Its branches filled the sky in all directions and then slowly diminished until only one branch was left. She stood at the end of the branch, waiting a little while for God, when a huge flash of lightning the color of grapes appeared, but no thunder.

The girl moved out of her bed toward the bathroom.

Silence could live in the night if it weren't for all the little sounds that the big sounds smothered during the day. There was the bed she got up from. And the water that stuck to her eyelids and creaked every time she blinked. Only God had no sound.

She stood to pray and then sat.

She had started staying away from noises to stay away from illness, and then in the same way, sounds began to stay away from her. At school no one talked to her, and at home she was no longer part of anything, as if she had had a huge fight with everyone and silence was the punishment. The silence stretched in every direction she looked. God removed Adam's and Eve's voices from Heaven, and in the same way, voices and sounds became removed from Him and forgot Him. But God was greatest in His silence.

Her head was bowed, lowering her sight to the floor tiles, which in the night had lost their shine to the stars. Dim light came only after adjusting to the dark.

Suddenly, two feet entered the empty space before her bowed head. The dim light detailed their swollen size and the rotting toenail on the right foot's big toe. On the way to the doctor, the little girl used to hold tight to the mother's dress and look at the ground, and the rotten toe would lead the way. Since she started going to the doctor by herself, the girl had not seen it.

The mother's two feet remained still, as if part of the silence that dwelled between the two. Often this silence felt like anger; the rest of the time, like heaviness. At any moment the mother might open her mouth, and thus lift the curtain for the entire household to watch the final scene in the saga of the illness that had begun in the ears and ended in the brain. At this time of night, sleep was better than prayer. Before the mother's mouth opened, the girl mustered up all her indifference. Silence could not be any more silent or any worse.

She lifted her head toward the mother, whose lips formed a long forgotten smile.

The mother's smile emerged silently, before the girl's prayers.

8 Inevitable

The call to prayer was like a fine powder silently sprinkled through the air.

The girl sat by herself on a metal bench big enough for two or three people. The right edge of the bench was parallel to the edge of the sea.

In front of her in the distance appeared the high seawalls and the waves' repeated attempts to climb over them. She took refuge on the only bench in the harbor to avoid getting splashed by the waves as they hit the walls.

As if that sea were not the same as this quiet sea beside her. The light that slipped into the darkness exposed the movement of a blue plastic bag inside the water. The plastic's movement was as supple as a mermaid's, and just as the mermaid's price for leaving the sea for dry land was eternal silence, so the bag's price for entering the sea was eternal silence. This was silence as a price. Another silence was a punishment from everyone, or, as in the case of the father, silence was inevitable.

As for the silence of her marriage, that was voluntary.

The call to prayer ended.

movement

I

The mother sat on a rocking chair that rocked back and forth until its movement faded away and she would start it up again. The little girl was standing in front of her on the edge of the veranda, holding onto its iron frame, while her eyes were fixed to the sky, holding onto the edge of a cloud. Thus her journey would start through the space over the veranda, with the mother behind her, until the cloud disappeared beyond the horizon. The girl would turn her head, then look straight up again and wait for the next cloud.

She suddenly got dizzy, so she sat on the edge of the veranda and pushed her head between the railings, but they did not allow it to pass through. Her head stopped just before the ears, and so did the spinning inside it. But everywhere else in the world, in the fields stretched out before her, the spinning continued. Millions of blades of grass were moving in the same direction as the clouds. The softness of the hair of that green sea was similar to the softness of the sun's rays the moment they spilled through the clouds.

From between the veranda railings, the wind blew over the grasses tenderly, turning them around, so that their greenness was less green. The little girl watched the color of the grass as it shifted way up to the end of the fields, or to the end of the wind.

She slowly pulled her head out from between the railings and started to look for the place where the mother's eyes were fixed. Before she could find it, the mother got up and the chair rocked nervously back and forth.

The mother did not perform the ablution because she had not touched anything foul since the noon prayer. She headed directly to the sewing machine, where she kept the tattered green prayer rug. The new red prayer rug was still in the closet, where it waited to come out on the two feasts—the short one and the longer one—of each year.

She picked up the two sides of the rug, flipped it into the air, then moved her hands away, letting it fall onto the floor freely. Sometimes one of the front edges would fold, and when she lowered herself onto the rug, she would fix the folded edge with a gentle movement that was not part of the prayer.

After "Glory be to my exalted Lord, Glory be to my exalted Lord, Glory be to my exalted Lord," the mother straightened her back, her hands withdrawing without any resistance along the entire length of the prayer rug, then raised all the way up onto her knees, where they remained. Their traces were left on the velvet where all ten fingers had passed. Ten velvety lines pushed the rug's soft hair backward, where the green was less green than in front.

The little girl followed the flow of lines down the length of the prayer rug all the way to the end of the field of green velvet, following the movement of the mother, as if it were the wind.

2

A long time ago, some shepherds had placed the trunk of a dead tree in the narrow neck of the valley to make it easier for them to move their flocks.

In the present time, the little girl stood on that same tree trunk, watching some tadpoles in the water. She tried to follow the movement of one tadpole, but she would lose track of it in the movement of all the others. Their movement was constant; she could not stop it.

She held her right hand over the surface of the water, so its shadow appeared in the bottom of the gray valley. Once again she examined the movement of the little creatures, but this time, above the large shadow of her hand. She lowered herself closer to the water, crouching like a frog. The shadow of her hand shrank, now containing within it the movement of only three tadpoles. When she brought her hand as close to the water as she could without getting it wet, its shadow contained the movement of only one tadpole. She tried to move her hand's shadow as quickly as the little tadpole, but the shadow lost its ability to distinguish between the many tadpoles, and it finally disappeared without catching any. The sun snatched the shadow from the valley, and the two left together at first behind the tree, then behind the mountain.

Despite being tired after her hunting expedition, the little girl could not keep her eyes off the constant movement of everything, so she clung to the cigarette of the father, whom she had found sitting on the veranda when she returned to the house. Between the father's silence and hers, the cigarette's smoke extended. The smoke came out as two puffs, one from the nose and the other from the end of the cigarette. The one coming out of the end of the cigarette rose at first in a line, then spread out to the sides, and its movement became like the movement of the smoke coming out of the nose. She chased the cigarette in the father's hand, trying to cut off the rising smoke with her fingers before it spread out in all directions. She tried hard to cut it off, but she could not stop the smoke, which curled around her fingers and continued to rise and disperse.

The movement of the smoke ignored the little girl's hand, just as the movement of the tadpoles had ignored its shadow.

3

When summers came, the green grass would wither in the fields, even though it was still rooted in the ground. Then the green machines would come to cut it. Although up close the yellow stubs looked soft as they shone in the sun, once feet began treading on them, their lack of softness became apparent. Even if the blowing wind turned into a violent storm, it would still be unable to move the yellow stubs like the velvety green fields.

The bales of hay were tossed onto the harvested half of the fields, and the shepherds headed there, with their flocks following behind, and dust behind the flocks, and behind that the road, the valley, and the mountain with all the balconies, observers sitting on them watching the entire outburst, which erupted the moment the harvesters left.

Everyone called the outburst revenge against the nature conservationists for prohibiting the free movement of the flock and the shepherds and sheepdogs.

The flocks dispersed across the harvested half of the fields while the children gathered near a bale of hay to decide when to begin moving, without involving the little girl, who stayed behind with the oldest shepherd boy to watch the flocks.

The sun was going down, and might disappear soon. Its trailing rays bobbed in the wind up into the big shepherd boy's nose, then into his eyes, forcing them shut.

The sounds of the children disappeared behind the bales of hay, and all that could be heard was the sound of the hay stubs beneath her bottom and beneath the shepherd boy's head.

The girl stretched her hand up toward the soft sky above her, but she could not feel it; it was too soft. Her feet, though, were crisscrossed with dry white lines that the coarse stubs had drawn on them as they touched.

The softness of the sky was above the softness of the sun, which was above the softness of the big shepherd boy's nose, and beneath him the hay stubs bent. A piece of hay almost entered his ear; it would, if he turned toward her.

The whole place seethed with waiting—the sunset for the sun's movement, the shepherds for the sunset, the herds for the shepherds, the big shepherd boy for the goats, and the little girl for the shepherd boy to turn his head.

The wait was over when revenge opened up onto the entire scene, with a secret movement.

The shepherd boy looked in the direction where the girl was not sitting, so the hay stub did not go into his ear after all. She moved to the other side and tossed her head very close to the golden nose. It was all she could see. Maybe the sun would push the shepherd boy's head again in the other direction.

As the secret movement began, smoke started to rise. She lifted her head and saw the source of the smoke spreading over the fields, gobbling up their yellowness, while the children jumped and cheered as they fled. Everyone saw how the secret movement had turned into a raging fire, all while the big shepherd boy's eyes remained shut. She moved to the other side and lay her head close to his, but still a patch of hay separated them. His breath snuck through the hay stubs to her face like the softness of the sky. She got closer. He did not back away, so she got even closer, until her mouth brushed against his two large lips.

The fleeing children reached them, so they got up and joined in, while the goats raced ahead and the mountain pulled the sun out from in front of them all.

Amid all the movement forward, the children checked behind them, afraid that the nature conservationists would discover their secret movement. Amid all the movement forward, the little girl looked back at the big shepherd boy, then forward toward the distant balconies, afraid that the people watching had found out about her secret movement.

4

A light drizzle hit the windowpane, sneaking stealthily from the opposite direction of the wind.

There were three windows and one door in the room, all shut, but the cold still got in. Calm prevailed. The teacher came in, but did not stay long. He put his hand to his nose and went back to the door, and with a kick opened it as wide as it would go before the floor caught and prevented it from moving further.

Calm lingered in the classroom, joined by the cold that came in through the door. The cold caused bodies to move involuntarily, and a few moments later so did a chair, then a desk and a mouth and so on. But everything came into stillness again when the teacher's head reappeared in the door. The head disappeared again, after forging silence with just one glance into the room, which was teeming with breathing and cold and flies.

The constant movement of the flies, which paid no attention to the cold or to the teacher, attracted the little girl's attention. She focused on one fly in particular as it jumped from one student to another, then onto her, then her desk, stopping to rub its front legs together before taking off to the back of the chair in front of her.

The girl tried to catch it in her small hands, but the fly was faster than she was. She tried again and nearly embraced it in her hands, but it flew away at the last moment. She tried again and again, until she felt a heavy touch on her back.

The teacher was standing behind her, holding the rubber tube and smiling. The other students were silent; then their mouths started moving. Everyone was laughing.

The girl started to run, wanting to get home before anyone else in the world. As she ran, she watched the speed of the ground below her. The rocks and little puddles and clods of mud and shiny wet dots of asphalt all looked just as they had traveling in the father's car.

She could see from a distance the mother, and the father's back. He was wearing the red scarf he always wore when it got cold. She ran toward him and jumped on his back. When the father turned his face toward her, the little girl saw the old neighbor's face. She got down off his back slowly, looking at his mouth and the mother's mouth, which were both full of teeth and laughter. The old neighbor had a knife in his hand, and between him and the knife was a chicken.

Laughter kept the knife shaking in the air for a long time.

5

The sky had not changed its silence or its shape or its position after the brother's soul rose up to it. The little girl raised her eyes to it, searching for some trace. She walked then stopped, ran then stopped, and finally she sat down. But the sky still looked the same, uninterested in all the movements underneath it.

She went back to the edge of the veranda and looked down at the ground. Beneath the ground the brother would be laid, and above the ground the visiting women sat.

She turned her eyes away from the women, toward the distant cars, which seemed slow. After seventeen he would come.

The seventeenth car left the main road and arrived at the dusty fig tree at the top of the road that led to the house.

The seventeenth car stopped in the courtyard. Its rear doors were opened and the brother was pulled out from inside on a narrow cot. The visiting women looked at the cot, then down at their feet. The shuddering of weeping came over them, and the shuddering of the cot carried on shoulders came over the brother.

The girl followed the cot as it was carried from the beginning until it reached the mother in the sitting room, where she sat all alone. The brother fell from the cot onto her lap. After some time, his face got wet because the mother's eyes were directly above it. Rather than wipe the wetness from her face, she wiped it from his. She moved her hands from the eyes to the cheeks, to over his mouth: over and over, slowly, as if she were playing *evol*. The gold bracelets were still dangling from her wrists. Each bracelet pushed the one in front of it until the final one touched the brother's face. Their slow touch must have been cold against his face. And they made a sweet sound when they tumbled on top of each other after any movement, even the slightest, in the darkness of the room.

The mother's weeping became a wailing, and the bracelets' slow movements onto the brother's face sped up. The sitting room filled up with the women and the sisters who tried to rescue the dead brother from the mother's arms. The harder they tried, the harder she held onto him, and he remained indifferent to all the movement around him.

6

A big mirror stood in the middle of the sitting room, and a little mirror was tucked inside the shaving kit hanging in the bathroom.

Every other day the father would sit down to shave. The little girl would bring one of the chairs and place it in the sitting room. Then she would get the shaving kit, take out the little mirror, and place it on the chair. Finally, she would go to the kitchen and come back with a glass filled halfway with clean water.

The water in the glass would get dirtier at the same rate that the father's chin got cleaner, aided by his hand tightly gripping the old brush. But a little bit of soap would remain under his ears. Then they both would sit down: he to eat breakfast and she to watch the bones of his face near his eyes move as he chewed.

The father would get into his car, without the girl knowing where he was going, even when she went with him. Sometimes she would go with him and sometimes she would stay on the veranda or in the house waiting for him to return.

The third sister would watch the father get into the car and move away inside it, leaving the courtyard behind empty. She would immediately run to the big mirror.

The big mirror stood there in the middle of the sitting room revealing the beauty of whatever went on in front of it.

No matter how long the father was gone, the third sister's hands would never stop combing. She would comb her hair once to the front, once to the back, to one side then to the other. Then she would stand in different poses, and other times she would make a hundred braids or a hundred and fifty. One time she made two hundred. She also had several bottles of nail polish, which she would put on then wipe off, making piles of colored cotton balls on top of the hairs that had fallen from her head to the foot of the mirror.

From the distance, by the window, the third sister appeared in her search for beauty to be dancing without music. The little girl watched her carefully from where she sat motionless except for the movement of her eyes from the third sister to the courtyard, over which the living-room window looked, waiting for the father's return. Sometimes, the third sister would move her eyes from the mirror to the same window, watching for the father's return before he could catch her doing the beauty movements.

7

The father had two pairs of shoes; one old and one new. When he was at home, the little girl wore the old shoes, which made her move slowly and clumsily. When she lifted one foot off the floor, it rose without the shoe, and when she ran, the shoes flew up in the air.

Whenever the father got ready to go out, he asked for the old shoes. That way the new ones stayed new.

Before she gave him the shoes, she picked up her little pair of shoes and, while he was busy pushing his feet into his shoes, she ran out to the car. When he went out to the car, he would find her there in the front seat, motionless and not about to move, her shoes in her hands.

From the car window, the girl watched the swift movement of the sidewalk bricks, which were no longer bricks, but lines. Above them was grass or dirt, which despite the speed still looked very much like grass or dirt. Then were the trees, like slow old ladies. And on the horizon beyond them the houses would not move until they were very, very far away.

As for the sun, sometimes it came to the front window or the side window and stuck to it. It did not move at all unless the day moved, and so the three passengers stayed together until they returned home.

The girl would get out of the car and start regaining her sense of walking again after the continuous sitting of their travels.

Her feet were weak and so the wind passing through the courtyard turned her stride into gentle swaying. It rocked her left and right, back and forth, until she reached the front step. Beside the step were the father's old shoes, which had arrived ahead of her. While she removed her own shoes and shoved her feet into the father's, the wind picked up again and fiddled with the olive leaves that had been heaped in a big pile by the family that had come to harvest the olives.

A mother and a father and then five daughters sat together at the end of the courtyard in front of the little house designated for them and for storing the harvest. They removed the leaves and sticks from what they had gathered in the morning, while the eldest sister combed her soft, black, very long hair incessantly in the same direction and with the same top-to-bottom movement, in front of everyone. Even in front of the father, who came sometimes during the day and sat near the family.

The eldest daughter kept combing her hair and tossing it from one side to the other, something the third sister had never done, until that day of that harvesting season. The father requested the old shoes, so the girl rushed to the shoebox to grab her little shoes and ran out to the courtyard.

The car was parked in the middle of the courtyard. The father was standing beside it, barefoot. Inside the car sat the eldest daughter, on the veranda stood the mother and the sisters, and in the courtyard stood the mother of the laborer family and her daughters.

The girl tried to get into the car, but the father pushed her away. She threw his shoes away and jumped into the back of the car. After the father put on his shoes, he climbed into the back of the car and carried her out. The mother yelled at him, and the mother of the laborer family yelled at the eldest daughter. The sisters stood there silently and the other girls stood there silently. And as soon as the father got into the car the girl got back into the car, and he got out and lifted her out again, got back into the car, and she climbed back in, and so on until the mother carried her away after she spat in his face.

Then the car started moving with the father and the eldest daughter inside, on their way out of the courtyard. The mother started moving, too, back into the house with the sisters following, and then the mother of the laborer family and the rest of her daughters started moving, into the little house.

And out came a loud scream.

Through the door in the middle of the little house someone was standing in midair.

Once the little girl's eyes adjusted to the darkness, she saw the father of the laborer family hanging by a rope tied to the ceiling. He swayed with the gentleness of the wind passing over him. It swung him right and left, back and forth.

8

The procession of women marched quickly in rhythm to the songs spilling off their tongues.

The girl was swept away in the movement of tongues and lips and the hands of the woman at the head of the procession beating on the drum, and the hands of everyone else in the procession clapping together.

No one knew how long the moment of farewell would last, but every movement was controlled and calculated whenever it happened.

Each sister, in birth order, passed by and embraced the bride, who was sitting by herself on the bridal seat. Her eyes embraced the white wall rising up behind the sisters.

Then they went out to the courtyard.

The girl lifted the skirt of her white dress, as her left hand held the bridal bouquet and the hair, and she pushed her right leg and her head through the car door that was open and waiting for her.

language

I

No matter how black the courtyard was, the shaded area would always be blacker.

For some time, the little girl had been standing in the same place watching her shadow and how it was moving closer toward her. The courtyard of the house was just like the schoolyard, except the shadow was different. In the schoolyard children were playing and jumping around, so one person's shadow got mixed up with another person's shadow and with everyone else's. There were many children, in the front and behind and on the sides. Children filled up all the corners and they pushed and shoved each other so their shirt buttons fell off and their words got mixed together. At school they also spoke differently from the people at home.

During the first Arabic class ever in life the teacher assigned the Lesson One dictation exercise for homework.

At home everybody was busy talking to somebody else. The girl waited for them to finish speaking in order to ask what the word "dictation" meant, but before they quit talking, the sun had quit the sky and she had fallen asleep.

Before the start of the second Arabic class, all the children copied Lesson One into their notebooks. The teacher inspected the notebooks, going from one desk to the next without changing the question, "Did you do the dictation by yourself?" And they answered, "Of course not. My brother dictated it to me."

The teacher arrived at the girl. At home everyone had

been busy talking with someone else or everyone else, and before they were free she had fallen asleep.

She answered, "Yes."

Her notebook got an X for wrong. Everyone else's notebooks got checkmarks for right.

The shadow got a bit closer.

In the courtyard the little girl yelled, "God damn!"

Just like the children said in the schoolyard.

2

The mother looked at the little girl's clothes and told her to take her coat.

The coat was black. The outside was leather and the inside was fur. All the other children's coats were cloth on the outside and cotton on the inside; among them she looked like a black sheep turned inside out.

So the girl would tell the mother, "It's not raining."

Halfway down the muddy road to school, the world would change color and start to rain, and so it would continue, endlessly.

Through time and repetition, the mother had learned to send the coat along with the neighbor.

The children gathered in the classroom long before the first class because it was raining and cold.

The girl looked at the rivulets of water streaming down the window, then approached it, puffed out a breath, and quickly wrote the words she had learned, watching them until they disappeared. At any moment the door might open to reveal in its rectangular opening the neighbor holding the black coat. He would come in, all eyes would follow his every move silently, he would place the coat on her desk, then leave, taking the silence with him, and incomprehensible chatter would return to the room.

On the way home from school all the children whistled at her and said the neighbor was in love with her.

The little mirror in the middle of the windshield did not show the drops of rain that had begun to fall on the courtyard, but it did show the absence of the sisters who had been playing there a few minutes earlier. Then water started to flow down the glass of the car window in distinct lines. The rain picked up until it coated the glass. Behind it the world altered its slant with every drop of rain, until the rain stopped.

The little girl opened the car door and walked across the courtyard, then over the mud to the tree near the neighbor's house. She went on waiting for him.

At first he looked slanted through the veranda glass, but the slant disappeared when he shut the door of the house behind him. Then the two of them shut the car door behind them, and they named their game *evol*, reversing the word *love,* to keep it secret.

3

Every night the little girl would go to bed at sleepiness's command, but this night she went to bed at the mother's.

From time to time, she would hear bits of words: "imals," "ker," "Allah," "dren," "tards," "ratila," through the door separating her room from the living room where the family had gathered. "Ratila" was especially difficult. Then she heard the television set click on, though the sound hardly made it through the door, but "ratila" became "abra and tila." After more repetition, "Sabra and Shatila."

Sabr was cactus, and cactus plants, wherever they would be found, were always the same, never decreasing and never increasing. So she did not know if *sabr:* cactus had a *shatla:* a seedling form. She slept until the sound of honey being stirred into milk woke her. She followed it into the mother's and the father's room.

The mother and the father had talked together since the night had begun to lift and until the sun arrived on the rug between their two beds.

Usually she did not understand their talk, so she ignored it and kept looking at the big picture hanging over the mother's bed. In the picture was a woman wearing a dark green dress that exposed her shoulders. She was picking light green grapes from a medium green vine.

When the sun came into the room, the father would turn on the radio between his bed and the mother's. But today the girl had been taken from the room to school before all of that. At school the children talked in a whisper so soft that the sounds of the birds could be heard over them.

The girl stood at the end of the schoolyard, looking down at part of a *sabr* plant the size of a donkey, which was blocked from view by a donkey standing in front of her. She stood there waiting for the donkey to go so she could store the missing part of the plant in her memory. The eyes fixed on the donkey were unable to prevent the ears from hearing a nearby conversation. "Oh my God." "Sabra and Shatila." "The pictures on the news." "How horrrrrrrrrr" rang the bell signaling the end of morning recess.

In the middle of class, a loud "Yeeeeeeee" rose out of the mouths of some of the students, and everyone turned toward it. The teacher came over it to the desk, on which the hands resting held a ruler with the word *Palestine* written across it.

The teacher gave the student a choice between erasing the word or throwing the ruler away in the trash bin in the corner. The student shrugged, the ruler still in his hands, like the woman with the bare shoulders holding the grapes in the picture above the mother's bed. When the teacher grabbed him by his shoulder, his shirt looked like the woman's dress getting snagged on a branch of the grapevine. The chair he had been sitting on crashed to the floor.

On the teacher's way to the door and then through it, as she dragged the student behind her by his shirt, she asked the girl to take her place until she came back.

The girl went to the teacher's desk, slid the chair out, and sat down. She looked at the students, and they looked different from when she sat among them, but confusion about what was happening made them look a little bit the same. She turned the chair around, giving her a view of the empty green board. The color of the woman's dress in the picture was like the color of cactus. The girl tried to understand the meaning of the words *Sabra* and *Shatila*. Maybe they were one word. The word *Palestine* was unclear, except that its use was forbidden. The color of the green board resembled the color of cactus.

She squeezed a piece of white chalk as if juicing a cluster of grapes across the board. "I am a donkey."

The students watched the little girl pick up the chalk, and when they read what she had written, they cursed her and decided to cut her off forever.

4

The little girl woke with the sound of onions sizzling in oil filling her ears and the smell of them filling her nose. She pushed the covers back and headed to the mother's and the father's room. Both beds were made.

Outside the siblings were lying down on the veranda. She asked them where the father was and they told her he'd left. She asked again, "Where did he go?"

"To Tallouzia,"* the brother answered. "But he said to tell you to catch up with him as soon as you woke up."

The girl watched the sisters' laughing teeth and tongues and the brother's mouth, which he reopened to ask if she wanted to go with him.

She asked, "To where?"

His answer was forever the same. "To the shit of Um Husein. I say ka-ka, you say fine."

She climbed onto the veranda railing and looked out at the road, searching for the father's car among the rest of the cars.

She tried to count how far away Tallouzia was. Thirty cars for the father's car to get there, another thirty cars for him to return, and twenty cars for his stay there. If he didn't come by then, she would count twenty more cars.

The metal railing was warm, so she pressed as much of her body against it as possible, continuing to watch the cars.

So far, twenty-five cars.

The warmth of the railing had changed to heat, as there were no more than three clouds in the sky.

* A made-up place name.

She looked behind her onto the veranda. The brother was stretched out on the floor, his eyes shut and his hands behind his head. The sisters' heads were all crowded together as they talked quietly, all except the second sister's head, which was behind an open book.

The veranda distracted her from the street, and counting the tiles beneath each body on the veranda took the place of counting cars on the street. The largest number of tiles was the brother's.

She returned to the empty road and the empty quietness into which, every once in a while, came the sound of a page being turned. Then the brother's voice returned to fill the quietness for a longer period, saying to no one in particular that he had heard the father saying he was going to bring the girl a bicycle. He added that when the father arrived with the little bicycle he was going to sit on it and it would break because he was so big and it was so little.

The giggles started up again.

She came down from the railing and went to the door. Before she shut it behind her, the brother swore he'd just seen a pigeon poop on her head.

On her bed, the little girl spoke to God, begging Him with all her might that He would agree, "Dear Lord, please make my brother die."

And the next day, her brother died.

5

After the funeral, the mother moved from the mother's and the father's bedroom to the sisters' bedroom and rarely came out of it. The sisters hardly left it either, so the house seemed as if no one lived in it.

During the first three days, the little girl came into the sisters' room whenever she wanted, and stayed a little while, looking at the mother's face or watching her pray.

The mother's grief and prayer mixed together; she wept when she was praying and when she wept, bits of prayers spilled out, as though the tears had erased some of the letters or words, as rain had once erased the girl's dictation notebook.

Every prayer ended with a plea for God to forgive the brother any offenses he might have committed and to grant him entrance into Paradise, after which the sisters said, "*Taqabbalallaa*."*

The girl did not understand this word, but she said it nonetheless, always last, because the sisters said it ahead of her. The eighth sister went first, and the mother responded, "From God and from you," warmly and slowly. The warmth went down and the speed went up each successive time until it was the girl's turn.

The sound of the door was loud when it was opened, as it struggled against the bedroom floor, which was scraped up with semi-circular lines, and when the door was shut, it didn't shut all the way. Even on the second try it might not shut. For her it would not shut even on the fifth try, so she slammed it, and it shut with a loud noise followed by familial sighs.

---

* To be accepted by God; said quickly as one word.

One day the mother complained.

Now the girl waited at the door until one of the sisters opened it to let her in or out. That way she would not harm the door anymore. Sometimes she waited from morning until noon. She heard the short chatter inside. "Enough weeping, Mother." "153." "Shhhhh. Mother's asleep." "Has your father returned?" "No." "Where's your little sister?"

She would answer from behind the door, "I'm here."

The mother no longer directed her speech at anyone in particular or mentioned anyone's name. Now she talked like the teacher when she gave lessons on pronouns. The sisters in the room: *you*. The little girl: *she*, even if she was in the room. And the father, now that brother was dead, had become the only *he*.

"Has she eaten anything?" "Yes."

The girl shouted, "No!"

"Feed her." Then, "You. No you. Yes… go… youyou yougoyesyou."

The door opened, so she tried to go in, but the eighth sister shoved her hard and she fell down on the floor. By the time she got up, the door was closed again. The desire to go in the sisters' room hung in the atmosphere all through the scooping of food onto the plate, the chewing of it, the swallowing, and even the washing of the plate. While the eighth sister washed, the girl waited right next to the door, stuck to it.

The eighth sister moved to the door and stood beside it, too. Then she leaned against it, turning her head from side to side and staring at the girl. Time passed between the eyes.

A blink could come at an unknown moment.

Suddenly the eighth sister pushed her to the floor. She landed on her elbow but did not cry out, so she would not make her mother upset. From where she was on the floor she saw the eighth sister open the door, so she summoned all her strength and lunged through the space between the open door and its being shut again, landing on the floor inside the room. The eyes and ears were many in the room, and all of them heard the shouts of the eighth sister. "I made food for her and then she came after me and hit me!"

She tried to say something, but the words disappeared and the letters were no longer arranged as before. There was her hand. She thrust her hand instead of the words at the eighth sister's hair, when suddenly the mother's hand was on her hair, dragging her out of the room.

"Out! She wants to kill me. I wish I would die!"

The little girl sat in front of the door, her throat filled with the loss of language mixed with the loss of being included in the pronoun *you*.

6

The once meaningless lines transformed into words that created worlds. Those worlds stood right behind the clean panes of glass.

The little girl started at the beginning, with the first book on the first shelf.

"Al. Alex. an. der. Dumas."

The Three Musketeers—1. Same name as the previous one—2. Then—3. The books were thick, so she went to the fourth one.

"Dos. Dosto. oevs. ski. yevski."

Crime and Punishment. Not as thick.

She placed her hand on the glass door to pull it open, but it pulled back on her. When she lifted her hand to try pulling harder, hand marks appeared on the clean glass. She quickly puffed warm breaths onto the glass and wiped the marks with her sleeve. The glass was clean again, and to keep it that way, the hand stayed inside the sleeve when she pulled again, and succeeded. Its sound was like that of a stone at the entrance to a cave.

She sat and put her face behind the book, waiting for the sound of the first page being turned to scratch the air in the room after a period of silence.

The first word went quickly; that was the father's name. After that, time moved slowly across the page. The words grew further and further apart, and more and more disconnected, but she continued nevertheless to try to read all the way to the book's distant end.

She read the word in its standard literary form and repeated it to herself in spoken dialect. Most of the standard literary words were close to the spoken ones, but there were three or four in each line that were incomprehensible, words she was encountering for the first time.

At first she tried searching among the things around her for meanings for the words, or for something without a name that might fit with the word, but spoken words had reached everything. The words without meanings increased until they filled the whole page, and she was no longer able to ignore them.

The little girl then started to picture something in her mind, then very quickly stuck the new word to whatever that was before a spoken word could reach it.

7

The books and the little girl went along hand in hand through the days, all the way to the third shelf.

She would lie on her bed, covering her body with a light sheet or a heavy blanket, and her face with a short novel or a long one.

The written words followed her eyes onto everything. Some book always stood between her eyes and all other eyes in the house, always hiding its world, which, if it appeared from time to time, appeared as a world whose words were read rather than heard, and so she did not say anything.

About the sisters she read on a sheet of paper or a diary carefully hidden under a mattress or in a drawer or behind a picture hanging on the wall. The father's world came from a little green box filled with papers, which was kept with other boxes full of tools for fixing the car. Shared events and similar feelings gathered in every diary and on every sheet of paper, transforming the single world of the house into several distinct, contradictory worlds, which the girl's eyes traversed. She read all the pages and reread them again and again. Without anyone seeing her, she came near each of their worlds, except the world of the mother, who didn't write. It was impossible to approach her unwritten world.

Nor did the mother know how to read, or she might have shared the girl's many worlds that existed in works on the first shelf, the second shelf, and halfway through the third.

Every new book and every new day increased the distance between the two. In the meantime, the mother waited for the girl to move the books out of the way between them, and the girl waited for the mother to read these books; the only time their two languages met was in an argument that accelerated their separation.

8

The mother said, "Father has been unfaithful to mother."
The father said, "Father has not been unfaithful to mother."

The girl did not choose sides. To the rest of the world, which chose the first option, this meant she had chosen the second.

Many days passed in which she didn't hear herself speak a single word. The only words were the ones she saw stacked neatly on the lines. But the choice between saying words and reading them was taken from her and became a punishment for not choosing sides. Her face had to be hidden behind a book. Just like that, with choice transformed into punishment, the abundant world behind the books became lonely.

Then one night, the glass door shut on the last book on the fifth shelf: *Learn Turkish in One Week*.

The girl lowered her eyes to the bookend of the first shelf. Alexander Dumas. The *Three Musketeers*, in three volumes. Against volume three leaned the first book, *Crime and Punishment*.

She left the bookcase and wandered around the house in the dark, but *Crime and Punishment* did not leave her. What kept reappearing was the murder of the woman, and the axe.

She sat near the fireplace, whose only warmth came from its dying embers, and listened to the sleepers' breathing. Some nights the eighth sister talked in her sleep, and even though what she said was incomprehensible, the girl listened to it carefully.

Now she listened closely to the mother's breathing, which continued without any break.

Between the house's sleep and the girl's sleep there was only night. Only the stars and the streetlights and some empty balconies remained awake. Between the dots of light, she stretched lines she could read, and above those words or below them, diacritical marks, disguised as shooting stars. And with the speed of a shooting star she also became the thief of her sisters' diaries, every night reading them and for every sister writing in them the words of the stars. But this had no effect on the daily and eternal punishment of silence.

The only time the punishment was lifted was when the mother got sick and the father went to the hospital. The girl then stayed with the sisters in the house. After a long time came the first exchange of words, in spite of the power of the silence. She asked, "Do you think my mother is going to die?"

The first sister replied by slapping her face.

The mark her hand left was hot and red like the wax used to seal letters. The heat of it on her face equaled the heat of the embers in the fireplace after she stirred them up. Someone else's hand swung the door to the sisters' room shut. Suddenly there came a voice close behind her.

The eighth sister said that she had been reading what the girl had written in her diary. They had all been reading what she had written. Their silence did not mean the absence of love, but the father's unfaithfulness was the absence of love.

The girl replied, "No."

No choice between the father's statement and the mother's, and no more writing in the sisters' diaries.

the wall

The bride sits on the bridal seat all alone, embracing the wall with her eyes.

Time passes and so do the sisters, edging closer to the end, while the girl's embrace of the wall intensifies.

Everyone is looking at her, and she looks back.

At the wall.

It encompasses all vision. Between the bumps on it, she strings lines in every direction, and the closer the end of the line of sisters, the harder she squeezes her fingers around the bouquet. Between the bumps she strings lines with her eyes. She cannot escape it.

They cannot wait any longer. The procession of cars must start moving.

The car rides into the distance with the girl as a bride inside it.

Her eyes are fixed on the rearview mirror, watching the house move away.